FOR FINNUR

x x x

First published 2023 by Two Hoots
an imprint of Pan Macmillan
The Smithson, 6 Briset Street, London EC1M 5NR
EU representative: Macmillan Publishers Ireland Limited, 1st Floor,
The Liffey Trust Centre, 117-126 Sheriff Street Upper, Dublin 1, D01 YC43

Associated companies throughout the world
www.panmacmillan.com
ISBN 978-1-5098-8986-0
Text and illustrations copyright © Morag Hood 2023
Moral rights asserted.

1 3 5 7 9 8 6 4 2
A CIP catalogue record for this book is available from the British Library.
Printed in China
The illustrations in this book were created using lino print and mono print.

www.twohootsbooks.com

MIX
Paper | Supporting
responsible forestry
FSC
www.fsc.org
FSC® C116313

DIG DIG DIGGER

MORAG HOOD

TWO HOOTS

It is a day like any other
at the roadworks.

"I DIG," says Digger,

"I ALWAYS dig."

"I don't like
digging any more."

Digger has heard of something exciting.
It is called UP.

And she really
wants to go.

Up would be sky,
stars and adventure.

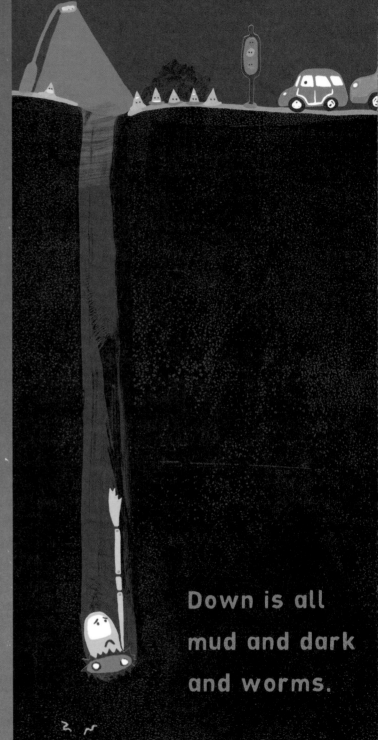

Down is all
mud and dark
and worms.

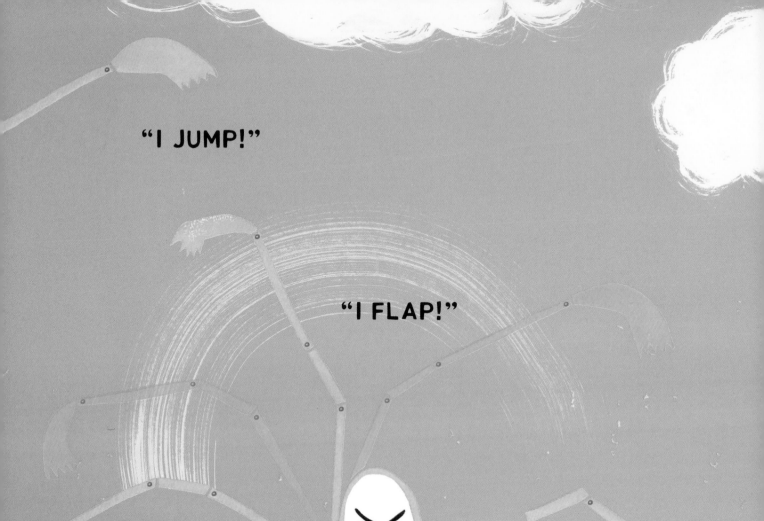

"I JUMP!"

"I FLAP!"

But then, when everything
seems lost . . .

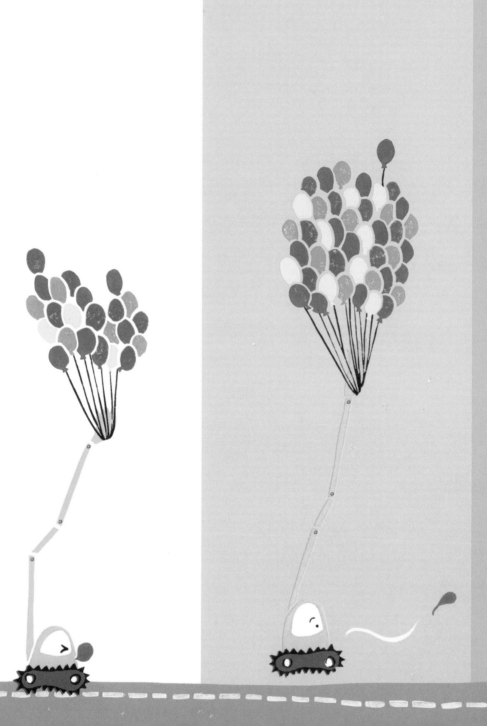

"I FLY!"

"Bye, Lamp-post.

Bye, Traffic Lights.

Bye, Big Car and Little Car.

Bye, Cones . . .

"I'm going on an adventure.

I'm going by myself!"

Up is exciting and blue.

But up is also far away and empty.
"I don't like up any more," thinks Digger.

Luckily, what
goes up,

usually does come down . . .

just not always where you want it to.

"I don't like soggy islands. I like friends."

It seems there is only one thing for this digger to do.

"I dig,"
says Digger.
"I dig DOWN,

and down,

and down
some more..."

DIG

DIG

DIG ...

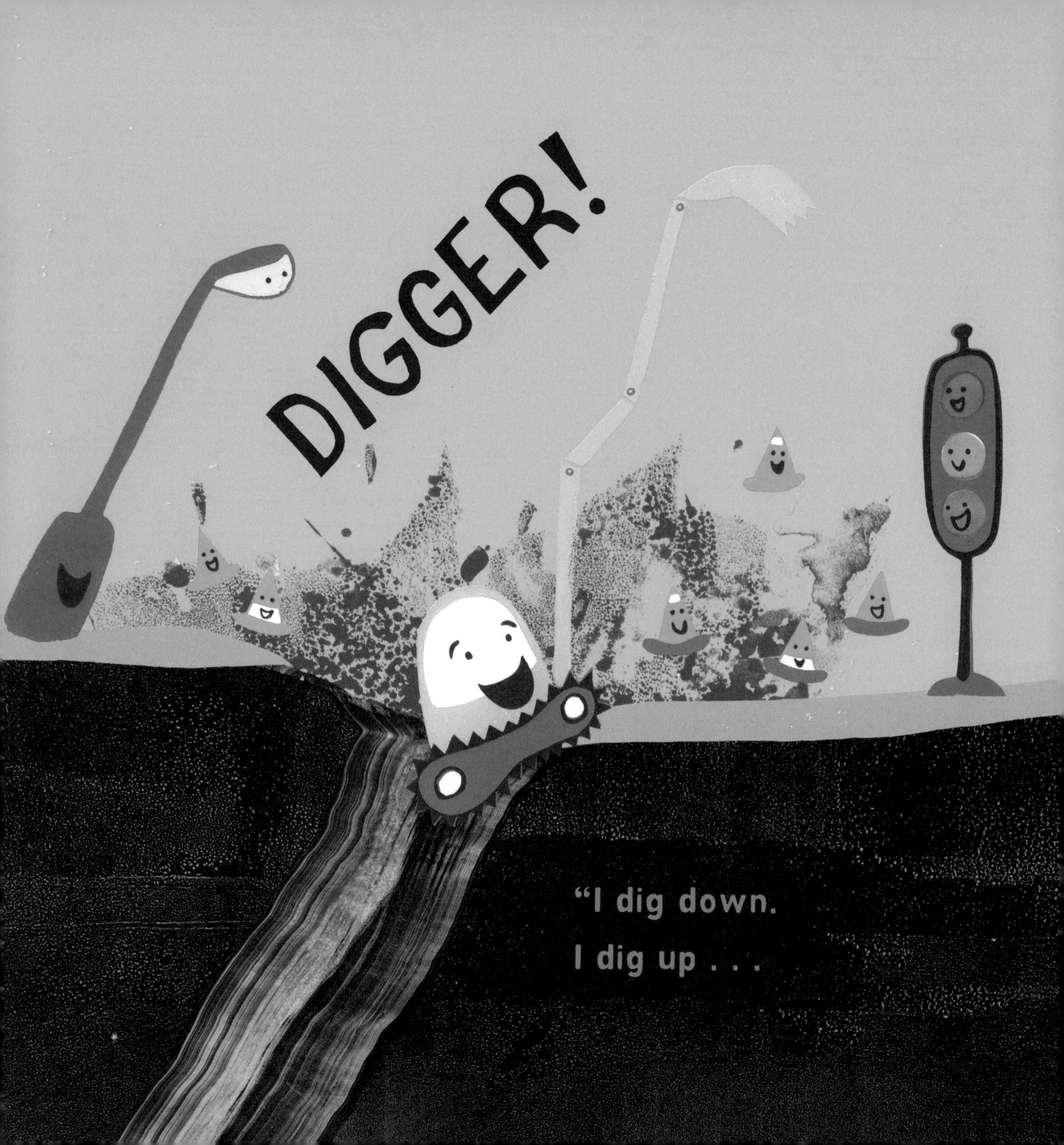

"I dig down.

I dig up . . .

"I dig home."

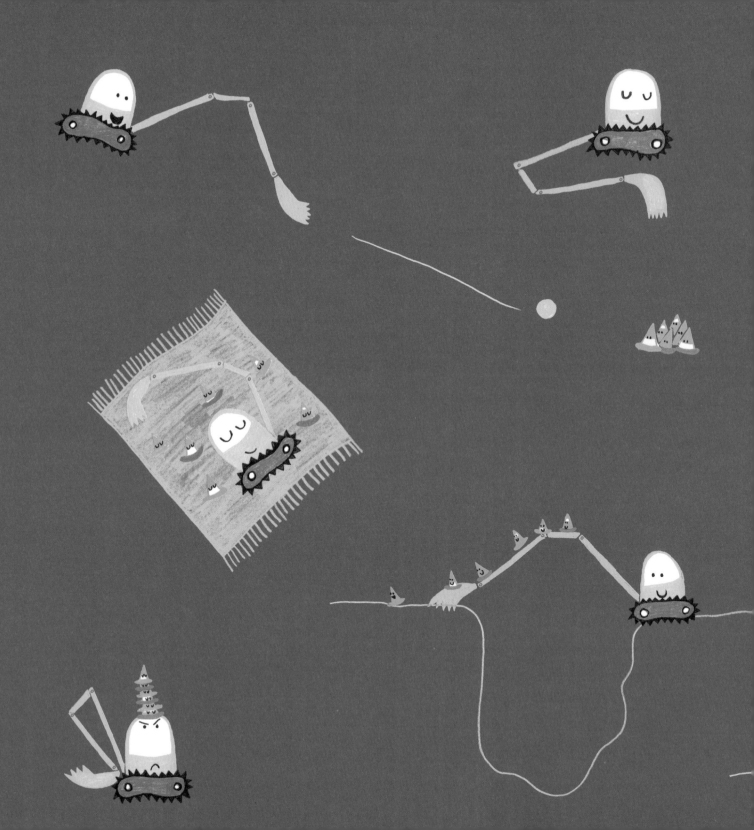